Ladybird Readers

The Enormous Turnip

Series Editor: Sorrel Pitts
Text adapted by Sorrel Pitts
Illustrated by Richard Johnson

LADYBIRD BOOKS

UK | USA | Canada | Ireland | Australia
India | New Zealand | South Africa

Ladybird Books is part of the Penguin Random House group of companies
whose addresses can be found at global.penguinrandomhouse.com.
www.penguin.co.uk   www.puffin.co.uk   www.ladybird.com

Penguin
Random House
UK

First published 2016
003

Copyright © Ladybird Books Ltd, 2016

The moral rights of the author and illustrator have been asserted.

Printed in China

A CIP catalogue record for this book is available from the British Library

ISBN: 978-0-241-25408-0

Ladybird Readers

The Enormous Turnip

Picture words

old man

enormous turnip

old woman

boy

girl

dog

5

The old man has
got some turnips
in his garden.

One turnip is very big.
"What an enormous
turnip!" says the
old man.

"I want this turnip for dinner," the old man says.

He pulls and he pulls, but the enormous turnip is too big.

9

"I want this turnip for dinner," the old man says to the old woman. "But I cannot get it. Please help me."

They pull and pull, but
the enormous turnip is
too big. They cannot get it.

13

"The old man wants this turnip for dinner," the old woman says to the boy. "Please help us."

They pull and pull,
but the enormous
turnip is too big.
They cannot get it.

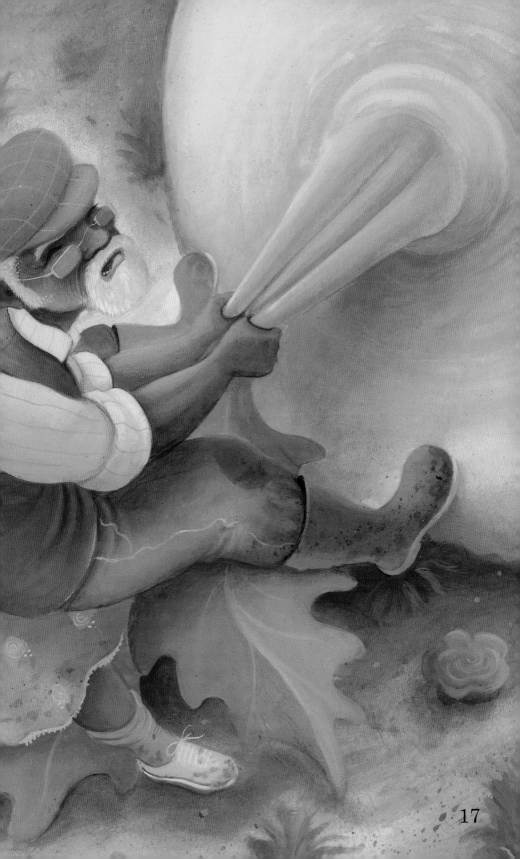

"The old man wants this turnip for dinner," the boy says to the girl. "Please help us."

They pull and pull,
but the enormous
turnip is too big.
They cannot get it.

"The old man wants
this turnip for dinner,"
the girl says to the dog.
"Please help us."

22

They pull and pull
and pull.

Now, the enormous
turnip is in front
of them! They are
very happy.

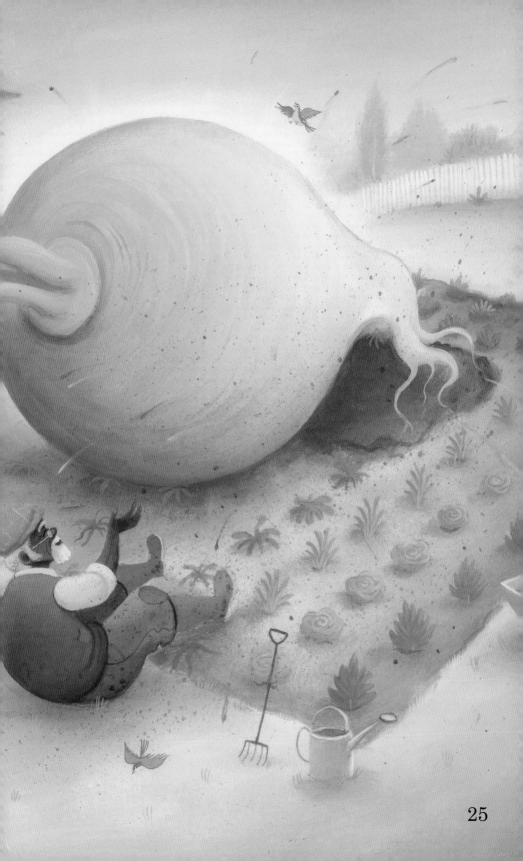

And they eat the
turnip for dinner.

Activities

The key below describes the skills practiced in each activity.

Spelling and writing

Reading

Speaking

Critical thinking

Preparation for the Cambridge Young Learners Exams

1

Look and read.
Put a or a ✗ in the box.

1  This is the old man. **✗**

2  This is the old woman.

3  This is the boy.

4  This is the girl.

5  This is the enormous turnip.

2 Look and read.
Write yes or no. 📖 ✏️ ⭕

The old man has got some turnips in his garden.

One turnip is very big. "What an enormous turnip!" says the old man.

1 The old man has
got some turnips in
his garden. ....yes.......

2 One turnip is enormous. ....

3 The enormous turnip
is very small. ....

4 The enormous turnip
is blue and yellow. ....

3 Look at the pictures. Look at the letters. Write the words.

1 n p t r i u

t u r n i p

2 e g d n r a

3 l u l p

4 l r g i

5 o g d

4 **Work with a friend. Look at the picture. Ask and answer Where? questions.** 💬

"The old man wants this turnip for dinner," the boy says to the girl. "Please help us."

18   19

Example:

> Where is the boy?

> He is behind the wall.

5 **Find the words.**

e	a	t	o	h	i
n	x	u	y	a	b
o	l	r	q	p	v
r	z	n	k	p	j
m	w	i	q	y	b
o	t	p	g	h	x
u	z	q	w	m	n
s	o	u	k	w	z
d	i	n	n	e	r

eat

dinner

turnip

enormous

happy

6 **Read and write the correct words.** 📖 ✏️

the old woman   the boy   the girl   the dog

1 First, <u>the old woman</u>
helps the old man.

2 Then, _____
helps them.

3 Then, _____
helps them.

4 Then, _____
helps them.

7 Work with a friend. Talk about the old man's kitchen. 💬

And they eat the turnip for dinner.

Example:

> Has the old man got a table in his kitchen?

> Yes, he has got a table in his kitchen.

8 **Circle the correct word.**

1 The enormous turnip is too big.
They **can** / **cannot** get it.

2 "Please help **them** / **us**," the boy
says to the girl.

3 "The **old man** / **old woman** wants
this turnip for dinner," the girl
says to the dog.

4 Now, the enormous turnip is in
front of **her** / **them**!

5 They eat the turnip for
breakfast / **dinner**.

9 **Ask and answer questions about the picture with a friend.**

Picture words

old woman

old man

boy

girl

dog

enormous turnip

Example:

> Where is the old man?

> Behind the enormous turnip.

. . . glasses?

. . . the enormous turnip?

. . . the old woman?

. . . the ball?

10 Write the sentences. 📖 ✏️

and pull They pull .

1 They pull and pull.

cannot they it get But .

2 ....

us help Please .

3 ....

very are They happy .

4 ....

eat turnip the They .

5 ....

11 **Ask and answer questions about the picture with a friend.** 💬

And they eat the turnip for dinner.

1

Is it morning or evening?

It is evening.

2 What is the old man doing?

3 How many people are eating?

4 Where is the dog?

12 **Circle the correct picture.**

1 Who has got a dog?

2 Who lives in the house next
to the old man?

a  b

3 Who likes playing football?

a  b

4 Who talks to the dog?

a  b

13 **Read and answer *yes* or *no*.**

1 Has the old man got
   vegetables in his garden? .... yes ....

2 Does his garden have lots
   of enormous turnips? ....

3 Does he like
   eating turnips? ....

4 Is the girl's dog brown? ....

5 Do the boy and the girl
   enjoy their dinner with
   the old man? ....

14 **Look and read.**
Write _yes_ or _no_.

"The old man wants this turnip for dinner," the girl says to the dog. "Please help us."

1 The girl is talking to the dog. .... yes ....

2 The dog is running.

3 The old man is sitting.

4 The boy is pulling the turnip.

5 The girl is wearing a green jacket.

15 **Ask and answer questions about the old man's hair and clothes with a friend.**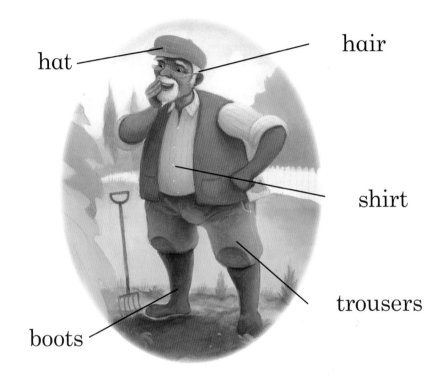

hat

hair

shirt

trousers

boots

Example:

What color are the old man's boots?

He is wearing green boots.

16 **Match the question to the answer.**

1 Who enjoys reading?

2 Who enjoys working in the garden?

3 Who enjoys playing football?

4 Who enjoys walking a dog?

5 Who enjoys eating with people?

a the girl

b the dog

c the old woman

d the boy

e the old man

17 **Order the story. Write 1—5.** 📖

_____ "The old man wants this turnip for dinner," the boy says to the girl.

__1__ "I want this turnip for dinner," the old man says to the old woman.

_____ They eat the turnip for dinner.

_____ "The old man wants this turnip for dinner," the old woman says to the boy.

_____ "The old man wants this turnip for dinner," the girl says to the dog.

18 Talk to your teacher about the turnip.

Example:

This is my garden.
It has got an
enormous turnip.

19 Read this. Choose a word from the box. Write the correct word next to numbers 1—5. 📖 ✏️ ⭐

> pulls   enormous   turnips
> says   house

The old man has got a garden behind

his ¹ ___house___ . He has got

some ² _____ in his garden.

"What an ³ _____ turnip!"

says the old man.

He ⁴ _____ and pulls but the

turnip is too big. "I want this turnip

for dinner," the old man

⁵ _____ .

Level 1

Anansi Helps a Friend

978–0–241–25409–7 ☐

Cinderella

978–0–241–25407–3 ☐

The Enormous Turnip

978–0–241–25408–0 ☐

On the Farm

978–0–241–25413–4 ☐

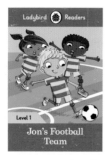

Jon's Football Team

978–0–241–25411–0 ☐

The Magic Porridge Pot

978–0–241–25406–6 ☐

In the Garden

978–0–241–26220–7 ☐

Fun with Old Things

978–0–241–26219–1 ☐

Peter Rabbit Goes to the Island

978–0–241–25415–8 ☐

Topsy and Tim Go to the Zoo

978–0–241–25414–1 ☐

Now you're ready for Level 2!

> **Notes**
> CEFR levels are based on guidelines set out in the Council of Europe's European Framework. Cambridge Young Learners English (YLE) Exams give a reliable indication of a child's progression in learning English.